Mark's Adventure

By Mary Starner

Copyright

First Edition: November 2015

ISBN-13: 978-1518685026

Table of Contents

Escape From Near Death

★ ★ ★ ★

Watching the familiar shape of earth recede on the viewing screen made Mark feel a little sad, but he was sure he'd made the right decision.

He was a very bright youngster, but boisterous with an impish sense of humor, who found school tiresome except for vacations. Mark knew his parents were disappointed by the low grades and teacher's comments on his messy, illegible papers, but he just couldn't settle down to the daily work. Why bother? He knew enough to get by!

When Mark and his classmates had been kidnapped by the Sularians, he had adjusted quickly to their pioneering life, finding it much to his liking. After returning to Earth, it didn't take long to find out that he'd grown up faster than of the children of his age. While many of his classmates were making plans to finish their interrupted educations, he knew he couldn't face several more years of schooling. Mark knew that some of the others wanted to return to Sularis after finishing college, particularly Ron and probably Barry. He didn't want to wait that long.

Many things had happened to his family during his years away from Earth and he felt it would never be the same particularly after his parents divorce. After several lengthy discussions lasting long past midnight, his parents had agreed to let Mark go back to Sularis if the screening committee accepted him.

Terrell, the wise leader of the science team in charge of monitoring the American children during their enforced stay on Sularis, agreed to sponsor Mark's return. The scientist had grown fond of the eager redhead who resembled the Sularians more than any other in the group of Earthlings he had watched for nearly five years.

Mark had passed the physical and psychological testing with ease and here he was finally on his way. He had watched with interest, the others being screened. Thousands had applied, filling out the lengthy questionnaires necessary for the narrowing down to twenty-five diplomats, scientists and news media people allowed to go on this first official trip to the newly discovered Sularis. No one with criminal records, chronic health problems or addictions, or heavy family duties were accepted. The very sophisticated physical examination cut the list even more, often discovering the beginnings of disorders the patients and their personal physicians hadn't suspected as yet.

The final examination was a thorough psychological profile used to drop those candidates who might be cruel, dishonest, overly ambitious, morally weak or prejudiced. Finally, the first group to represent Earth on Sularis had been chosen, briefed, packed, and ready to go. Mark, who had kept his intentions secret from all but his family and the Sularian selection committee, said his quick farewells to his astonished and envious friends.

Now here he was off into space again, eager to start a new life on another planet. He had one advantage over all the others in the group. He had been there before.

The required deep sleep period was actually a relief to Mark. The last days before departure had been tense and hectic. Though happy with his choice for the return, leaving his family and friends behind was harder than he thought it would be. Gratefully he accepted the medic's attentions and relaxed into temporary oblivion.

Even though he'd seen it before, Mark was just as excited as the other passengers when they were awakened to see the approach to the earthlike planet and to watch the landing on the view screens.

Because he had a sponsor and was known to the Sularian government, Mark didn't have to go through the lengthy, formal welcoming ceremonies and customs screening. Kayla had come to greet him with an offer of guesting privileges at her home, but Terrell had already made arrangements for Mark to stay with his family. It was convenient for Mark. He'd been hired as an archeological technician apprentice for one of the government teams mapping the vast unexplored areas of the large planet.

Sularis was newly colonized; a planet four times the size of Earth. Its vastness was untouched by other sentient beings as far as the preliminary survey scouts had been able to determine.

The scientific teams responsible for its exploration were expected to do their jobs while disturbing the natural environment as little as possible. The colonies grew in a carefully planned manner to follow this directive as well. Thus, the knowledge of their new home came slowly and there was much to discover. The first colonists had been chosen on their home planet as carefully as had the newly arrived representatives from Earth, so the social atmosphere was one of friendly ease and cooperation. Mark was very glad to be a part of it again. After a few days of visiting with friends and settling in, he was eager to get started on his first job assignment.

He found to his chagrin that classes would be necessary, as would a series of immunization shots to protect him from unknown diseases and accidental food poisoning in strange territory. Mark, himself, would be something of a guinea pig. These vaccines and antitoxins had not been used on Earthmen before.

That first day was a blur of activity as Mark filled out forms, took written exams, and met his superior officers and teammates. He was issued uniforms and equipment and finally scheduled for tutoring and training sessions. He was drawn immediately to Scagen, a boy just a few years older and six months advanced in his training. Scagen was to be Mark's tutor and general guide until Mark could catch up with the group. A red-head as were all Sularians, Scagen had a quick sense of humor tinged with a bit of the ridiculous that immediately struck a responsive note with Mark. However silly he might appear, Scagen was quick, reliable and dedicated to his career. Like Mark, he was training to be an archeo-tech, searching out any clues of past ancient history on the planet.

To his surprise, Mark found he was a good student after all! He looked forward to his classes, all of them, not just the physical training given for the hiking, mountain climbing, and survival techniques. The weeks passed very quickly as he immersed himself in the stimulating studies of archeology and the ecology he once thought a deadly bore. He didn't have to worry about submitting papers or laboriously taking illegible notes. The Sularians provided him with mini tapes and a reader for study, and an ingenious device for taking notes. Even more interesting were the history tapes, which covered the fifty years to the present, from the first colonial ship to the latest election in Sula, the capital city. Now he would be a part of that history as the first colonist admitted from Earth.

Being a pioneer was nothing like the old west days. The Sularian colonists had brought with them the latest, most modern inventions and information available on their home planet. All of the first colonists had been chosen so that each one had several skills and special knowledge for all the necessary professions such as agriculture, medicine, education, and the various sciences, as was a large group of technicians and a common labor force. An excellent education system prepared the children to take their place in the growing society. Expansion over the planet was taking place slowly. The colonists worked with nature rather than taking advantage of what the planet had to offer, ruining it, and then trying to replace what was lost.

It was the job of the governmental exploration teams to open up new territory. First the aerial photographers and the geologists did a preliminary survey. Then the ground teams went in for more detailed exploration, operating out of strategically placed semi-permanent base camps. Mark, at the end of his training, would join one of the smaller teams. His particular specialty was watching for and investigating signs of possible intelligent beings or hints of long gone ancient civilizations which may have existed in the past. Sularis was a planet rich in nature's gifts and it was unusual that it seemed devoid of any intelligent life.

Mark worked diligently to catch up to his classmates, with the help of Scagen, already his best friend and Kayla's encouragement. Mark soon managed to make up the work he missed by entering the class later than the others. Now the threesome had time to worry about the coming assignments. Kayla was already a trained com-tech and had passed her probationary training period. She had almost lost her place in the agency because she had been careless while on watch over the unsuspecting Earth children confined in a secluded valley. She'd allowed them to escape before her superiors had wanted them to come into contact with the Sularians. Kayla had been the first to meet the kidnapped group. Mark a member of the class of Earth children, was the one she felt most comfortable with, initially because of his red hair, later because they seemed so much alike. Both were fun loving, mischievous youngsters, indifferent, messy students who had much to offer and were whole-heartedly behind anyone or an idea. Kayla had been severely reprimanded and set back on the promotion list for her offense. Now, at last, she seemed to be back in the good graces of her superiors.

The ideal assignment would be all three on the same team but they hardly dared hope for that! Everyone at the academy talked more and more about the number of possibilities. The latest grades and qualifications were fed into the computers and the results tabulated, but their instructors were maddeningly slow about posting the assignments.

Terrell decided on taking a second chance on Kayla. After all she was an excellent communications technician and at least three were needed at his base camp. Mark was chosen for one of the smaller teams assigned to Terrell's expedition. That was a plus because Terrell was a good friend as well as his sponsor. There was much groaning and crossing of fingers among the three as they waited to hear about Scagen' assignment. As luck would have it, his name was nearly the last one announced and they nearly died of anticipation before "Scagen" was called. He'd drawn the same assignment as Mark! All dignity was lost for a few minutes as the two young friends jumped up and down, pounding each other on the back. Only the stares of the older cadets kept Mark from doing an improvised wild dance complete with warbling call.

The Expedition

★ ★ ★ ★

Terrell's expedition set up base camp at the foot of the immense, brooding Clacton Mountain Range which stretched like a giant wall to divide the continent nearly in half from ocean to ocean. Between that barrier and the last settled outpost lay miles of rock jumbled badlands. Promising ore deposits had been spotted by the airborne geologists in that area. One team was to work back and forth towards the settlement through the grey, rocky desert.

Terrell was to remain in command at the base camp to coordinate the incoming reports, relaying the findings to headquarters. Mark and Scagen were assigned to the climbing team which was to try scaling that formidable, mountain barrier. At the last minute Kayla was added to the team because of the strange communications difficulties the survey pilots had encountered when flying in that area.

Their assault on the mountain was set for the next day. The hours of preparation in the past weeks had often been spent studying photographs and the few sketchy maps available for the easiest possible route toward the most likely pass. For now they were to be content with gaining the peak to study what lay on the other side through the distance lenses. No descent on the other side of the range was planned. Turbulent winds and thick cloud cover had prevented survey pilots from making more than a few high level passes over the territory. They were heading toward an area of complete mystery.

It didn't take long to discover that the specially designed creeper could only haul supplies a short distance up the mountainside. Gunther, the team leader, ordered the many provisions and equipment cases back-packed to the cave picked for the first mountain base camp. This took many more days than they had planned, of grueling, back-breaking, muscle-cramping climbs through slipping gravel and over rocky outcrops. Gunther urged them on, jokingly reminding them that this was only a training exercise for the main event. Even Kayla had to carry her share. They were eager to get to the rest of the ascent working from first light to well after dark. Any real hiking on the treacherous path was done only in daylight. Stowing gear and making the roomy cave livable to a small degree could be done by perma-lamp. Sketchy meals and exhausted sleep followed.

After the last of the supplies were hauled up and stashed away, the party took a day off to rest before beginning the more difficult part of the climb the next day. Three days should bring them to the foot of the pass if the struggle through the increasingly rarified air went as planned. In the end, it took nearly double the time. Distances at this height were deceptive and rock formations more difficult to get up, over or around than they had expected. One of the men slipped and broke his leg in several places and the medic with two helpers had laboriously carried him back to the cave to await a rescue party from Terrell's camp. It was an increasingly gloomy, exhausted party of climbers who finally reached the beginning of the pass only to find nothing but clouds visible between the peaks.

"We'll camp here for the night and try to go through to the other side tomorrow," Gunther ordered. "Perhaps the clouds will be gone in the morning,"

"Sir, I'm having trouble contacting the base. My equipment isn't functioning properly," Kayla called. Investigation and testing found no observable problems with the equipment itself. It appeared that the interference might be a natural part of the mountain range. Air survey units had noticed interference with instrumentation and communication when they braved the dangerous air turbulence to come closer to the mountains.

"We'll have to use visual signals as planned Kayla," Gunther replied.

Shelter was soon arranged under a rock overhang to the left of the pass. Here, two gigantic boulders seemed to wall off the direct force of the ever-present wind which howled and blew most through the pass itself. Somehow, the small fire brought more than warmth to the party huddled around it. The brightly flickering flames helped to dispel the gloom and cheer them up a little.

It was the necessity for getting out of the cutting wind that probably saved their lives. Just before dawn, they were awakened by the shaking and roaring of a massive rockslide that crashed and rocketed about them. The awesome silence and the utter dark that followed was finally broken by Gunther softly calling roll. All answered except Ross and Kayla. Cautiously moving inch by inch so as not to disturb another rock fall, Mark was finally able to locate his perma-lamp and turn the beam carefully around their partially buried campsite. Kayla lay in her sleeping bag at the farthest end of the sheltering ledge, unconscious from a glancing blow. A large rock had apparently ricocheted backwards, striking her. No trace of Ross could be found. Nothing much could be done until daylight and they could see to move cautiously. No one wanted to risk starting another avalanche.

Thilker, the medic, was able to ease his way to Kayla.

"She seems to be out from the blow but otherwise okay as far as I can tell now. I'll stay with her until it's light rather than try working my way back."

No one really slept for the remaining hour before first light revealed a greatly altered landscape. It was as if the mountain itself had moved to block the pass. It no longer existed except as a frozen sea of tumbled rubble that reached almost to the peak itself. The slide had also obliterated the trail they had so laboriously fashioned on their way up.

Kayla came to with a king size headache and lump to match but assured them all she had no other injuries. She was ordered to rest where she was while the rest of them made a careful search for Ross. It wasn't long before they realized they would never find him. He had been a loner who always parked his sleeping arrangements a little distance from the rest. The night before, he followed that habit, moving off a little around the side of one of the two giant boulders forming part of their refuge. Jammed debris now filled that space to the top of the boulder itself. They dared not risk the lives of the others to probe or move any of that pile to find Ross.

Scagen volunteered to pick his way carefully to a spot where his visual signals could be seen. Mark watched his friend out of sight at the end of the safety line before he turned to help put some order into what remained of their supplies. This didn't take very long so they settled back to wait for Scagen's return. Most of them dozed but Mark, anxious for his friend and bored by the forced inactivity, took the distance lenses and idly scanned the tumbled scenery before him. Panning to the left, his attention was caught by an interesting formation. He crawled cautiously to stand and rest his elbows on a large rock lightly, steadying the lenses for a better look. At a little distance, over the jagged debris to the base of a sheer cliff, there appeared to be a ledge wide enough to lead toward the top of the mountain. From where he stood, it looked almost like a ramp or roadway. Though he knew how deceiving the terrain had been up to now, this might be a good way to try if Terrell gave them the signal to continue.

As Gunther was about to send a scout along Scagen's safety line, the plucky volunteer returned gingerly inching his way across the loose scree. After resting a few minutes, he was able to relay Terrell's message. The choice of continuing their assignment was up to Gunther. He, in turn, felt that each member should have a say in the decision.

"If we go back now we'll only have to start all over from the bottom. It's dangerous, but at least here, we're more than half way," Mark reasoned. Most of the others agreed. Kayla was rapidly recovering and not many of their supplies had been lost. Only the medic took the other side of the argument.

"We've lost one man and injured two others. Perhaps we should go back, regroup and rest awhile before attempting another climb."

They finally persuaded Thillker to see their point of view and it was decided to continue the try for the summit next day. The pass had to be abandoned as it really did not exist any longer and was too dangerous in its altered condition. A signal flare was sent aloft to let Terrell know of their plan.

All checked their equipment, ate a skimpy cold meal, and turned in to rest uneasily for an early start the next morning.

As soon as it was light enough to see, Mark pointed out to Gunther the ledge he had noticed earlier.

"It might serve as a way up, sir."

"Getting across to the base of the cliff is going to be the hard part. That whole slope may shift at any moment. Still, it looks like the most direct path if we can make it."

Since it was Mark's suggestion he felt he ought to volunteer to be the first across the unstable mass of rocky debris before them. He shrugged into the straps of his pack, settled it firmly, fastened his safety line, and worked his way up and over the first large boulders barring his way to the deceptively even slope before him. Mark angled carefully upward, stepping gingerly each time, fearing his weight might dislodge enough of the loose debris beneath him to start another massive slide. Though the sun was hardly above the horizon, he soon began to sweat. Midway to his goal, one large boulder seemed to be anchored more securely than the rocks beneath him, so he paused to rest and give a small wave to the group watching him anxiously. A few minutes of rest and a quick appreciation of the panoramic view before him and he started again. It took him nearly two hours but he finally reached the firmer footing at the base of the cliff. He looked back to see that someone else had started to follow his line. Mark quickly anchored his safety line, slipped off the pack, and used it to lean against as he sat and watched the others. Like a column of ants, they inched their way across the route he had followed. He wondered if the observers at the base camp in the valley below could see this tiny line of dots moving across the newly formed slide area. With the guide line in place the rest followed at a slightly faster pace than Mark had managed. Still, it was well past noon before all of them were safe on the more solid footing near the sheer cliff.

The mountainside here seemed to be formed in giant slabs that appeared to fault in massive slices slightly tilted to an almost vertical plane. Mark's 'roadway' was a ridge formed by the top edge of such a slice. If they had been ants, it would be like working their way across the top of a piece of toast standing on edge. There would be no way of knowing, until they tried, if they could reach the peak this way. It seemed the only way open to them now.

More massive boulders lay tumbled in their path, but less than an hour's worming through crevices and scrambling over the tops of the giants barring their path, and they reached the 'roadway'. Climbing upward was easier but they had to take great care to avoid stepping on loose gravel. Even the tiniest slip might throw a person enough off balance to fall off the narrow ledge to an agonizing death on the jagged rocks below.

When they realized they would not gain the peak before nightfall the search began for a safe campsite. There was little shelter from the constantly whistling wind nor any wider spot to pause for long. In the end they had to stop where a crosswise slip of the slab had caused an outward bulge of the fault. Whether it was or not, the ledge appeared a little wider and the small thrust of the cliff wall did cut the wind somewhat. Kayla tried the portable mini-com but found its transmissions still blocked. Their visual signals were not answered either, making them feel even more isolated. After a quick meal of concentrated nutrients, each huddled into the warmth of the anchored sleeping bags to fall into exhausted slumber.

Scagen was the first to waken when the rays of the rising sun beamed into his face. He awakened the others and after a hasty breakfast of more tasteless tablets and a short slurp from their canteens, they packed up for a renewed attack on the upward trail. As hard as the climb was, everyone was eager to keep on. No one knew what exciting discovery might be around the next boulder. Leaving the shelter of their little corner brought them to a horrifying sight. If they had blundered on last night, all would have been lost. Just beyond their resting place the ledge simply ceased to exist. They had reached the end of Mark's 'roadway'. It looked as if all they could do was to painfully retrace their steps. Stymied!

Scagen was unwilling to give up so easily. "If the rest of the cliff fractured the way the part we are standing on did, why couldn't there be another ledge above us?"

"Well, fly up and take a look you goose," griped a dispirited Kayla.

I'll do better than that. I don't have to fly; I have an eye in the sky," he quipped with a grin. Taking his small signal mirror he fastened it to the telescoping antenna of the com unit. This he fastened to his collapsible tent pole and gave to the medic, the tallest in the group, to extend above his head. The contraption just barely cleared the edge of the cliff above them. A large rock was passed carefully from person to person and after the medic stood on that the improvised telescope cleared the edge.

"O.K. wise guy, how are you going to see into that tiny mirror way up there," Kayla asked.

"With my trusty spy glass matey!" Scagen used his distance lenses to focus on the view in the mirror while Kayla and Mark kept him from toppling over the edge of the narrow ledge they were so precariously perched upon.

"There is another ledge up there and it may be wider."

Gunther took a look and agreed that a usable ledge did exist. The problem was getting to it.

It took hours of perilous struggle to set a hook and inch their way up the cliff face to the dubious safety of the next ledge, but one by one, they finally made it. The effort drained their energy in the thin mountain air. After a brief rest, they toiled upward again. This time, their struggles were truly rewarded as late in the afternoon they reached the top of the mountain. Before them was an astonishing sight. As far as they could see to the very horizon stretched an immense, intensely green forest looking like an ocean of enormous trees. It was a view of incredible beauty. Whether this was a forest on a vast mesa or trees of varying heights in a giant crater they did not know. It was a temptation to find a way down immediately into that sea of comforting green after days of dusty shades of greys and browns, but their orders were to get to the top and not explore further.

Communication still seemed impossible and from this angle and distance, visual methods did not work either. After a nights rest, they would have to start down to make a full report. Scagen, using his lenses, sighted an aerial survey copter over the desert area and urged Kayla to try relaying a message through the pilot to Terrell. It took some time to catch the pilot's attention. Then they were able to get an abbreviated report through to base and receive a "Well done-return to base." reply.

They were all disappointed at not being able to go at least a little way down into that marvelous forest which lay so temptingly before them. Terrell was right of course. Their supplies were limited. They might not be able to return to the top of the ridge once they were in the forest.

As the summer season drew to its end, they risked running into more severe weather.

Just over the crest and down a few feet, all violent wind seemed to cease. Gunther allowed them to make camp there in a wide sheltered spot near a descending ledge. There the group rested, sweeping the tops of the trees with lenses for any glimpse of living creatures. Some new birds were sighted and logged. Mark asked permission to descend just a few feet where he thought he might be able to snag a piece of tree branch to take back for classification. Gunther rather reluctantly agreed cautioning Mark to be very careful. He slipped off his pack and with Scagen following, worked his way down to the tip of the nearest tree. Not close enough, a few more feet would do it.

"Mark, watch out for that green moss on the edge. It looks slippery," Scagen warned.

His warning was a shade too late. In his eagerness, Mark had been a little hasty and this one misstep proved to be disastrous. His foot slipped on the moss-covered edge of the cliff, flew out from under him, and he toppled over the edge and into the branches of the tree. Scagen saw Mark's fall momentarily halted before he disappeared in the branches below.

The Unknown

★★★★

Bouncing from one fragrant trampoline to another, Mark fell for what seemed like hours, before he slid unhurt off the last branch into the cushiony moss at the bottom of the tree. The cliff rose in a sheer sheet of unclimbable smoothness to his right as he sat up in the dim light. Sunlight didn't reach to the ground past the giant trees. Mark's first thought was to make the others aware that he was safe. He suspected correctly that at this distance and with the trees to muffle it, his voice could not be heard. His pack was back with the others. Fortunately, all techs on assignment wore equipment belts and the specially designed jacket's many pockets were filled with small useful items. It was the barest of survival equipment but it might make the difference for the boy who was now on his own in a completely alien environment.

Mark took out the small signal rocket and set it as close to the cliff side as he dared. He hoped that it would be able to clear the tips of the branches and follow the rock up high enough to give the flared signal to the rest of the party meaning he was alive and unhurt. It was foolish to hope they would risk the rest of the party to attempt his rescue now. At least they would know that he was o.k. He waited near the base of the tree for several hours so see if any sign came from above but at last he gave up. He had thought at first of trying to climb back up but found that impossible without the proper equipment. The first large branches were too far above the ground to reach with the length of fishing line attached to the end of the thin, tough coil of climbing rope attached to his belt. The trunk of the tree was far too large around for him to loop his rope to climb. None of his meager equipment could be pounded or forced into the dense bark of the tree to make an improvised ladder.

The need for water soon turned Mark's thoughts away from that route of escape. Even without sunlight, which didn't reach the ground, the undergrowth was thick beneath the trees. It was nearly impossible to catch a glimpse of the sky even by looking straight up. The green gloom should have been frightening but though unfamiliar it was not threatening.

Mark had two choices. He could travel following the cliff in either direction and hope to find water or go deeper into the forest itself to hunt for a spring. If he was successful in finding a mountain stream and following it he might reach the ocean. If he struck into the forest he might find more food available as well as water. He had Sustain tablets to last for two weeks if he rationed himself strictly.

It seemed to be growing darker, though it was hard to tell in the dim light of the forest. By his watch it should be about nightfall. Nothing to do now but squeeze himself into some fairly protected spot and sleep until morning. He crawled behind some low growing bushes against the cliff base and dug himself a little nest by hollowing out a space in the humus. From the zippered pocket along the bottom edge of his jacket he pulled out the waterproof bag that would turn the jacket into an emergency sleeping bag. Lightweight as a spider web, the special material would keep him dry and warm but it did not cushion so he'd have to endure the lumpy ground for his mattress. By the time he finished snuggling into his hood the only part visible was his face giving him the appearance of a large green grub.

The next morning he built a small stone marker to hold the message telling any possible rescuer that he had gone southwest to follow the cliff to the ocean. Thirsty but nourished by the one Sustain tablet he'd had for breakfast, Mark started on his search for escape and water. He wasn't too successful and curled up thirstier than ever that night. Still struggling through the underbrush and trying to follow the sheer rock barrier the next day, he saw the dark stains of past waterfalls on the cliff side. There appeared to be a dried stream bed leading for a short distance into the forest where it suddenly stopped. Mark grabbed a stick and tried digging in the shadiest spot at the end of the watercourse. The sand did seem more damp so he kept on but he didn't find water. He did find some small succulent type plants from which he wrung some rather bitter liquid. It quenched his thirst from unbearable to at least endurable. He hoped that all those immunization shots worked because he had to take risks to stay alive. There did seem to be a game trail of some sort to his left. Perhaps that would lead to another waterhole. Before he left that spot, he marked his trail again.

Cautiously Mark eased into the leafy green tunnel in the underbrush. So far he had not seen any animals nor any signs to mark their presence. From time to time he thought he heard birds but they too were invisible. The going here was fairly easy and the trail sloped downward. Perhaps it would lead to a river.

At a few places along the way he had to bend or crawl to follow the faint trail but often he found the bushes high enough to permit easy walking. If it weren't for the pressures of thirst and hunger Mark would have relished the solitude. There was a quiet beauty, an indescribable serenity to the forest surrounding him. Once his eyes grew used to the dim light, he could distinguish more than tree trunks and brush. Pale flowers gleamed here and there. A closer look revealed a lively insect world. He was even able to find some edible berries to supplement his Sustain tablets.

He had made a good choice when he decided to follow the slight trail. On the fourth day he came to a small spring bubbling out of the ground amid a jumble of rocks and brambles. He startled the first small animal he'd seen as it was drinking. The swift, soft creature with large brown eyes reminded him a little of earth rabbits. Somehow just seeing another living creature made him happier.

"Steady little fella, I won't hurt you," he crooned. Amazingly the timid creature ventured back to finish its drink and then sat back to groom its damp whiskers before giving Mark a long look and hopping off. Mark drank his fill slowly and washed his dusty face in the little pool before filling the small plastic waterskin from his survival belt and starting on his way. The pool emptied into a tiny brook which flowed on down the hillside. The game trail did not always follow the water course so Mark left that path. At the last minute he turned back and again left a small pile of stones with a note to show his new direction.

Again he congratulated himself on his choice for the tiny brook led into a larger rill. He might find a river yet. He found something more interesting and mystifying than a mere river.

Mark quickened his pace as he approached a clearing. Here, the last rays of the setting sun were touching the tops of the trees. This meant that during the daylight hours the place would be sunny. A welcome thought after days of the subdued gloom under the trees. He walked to the far edge of the clearing and saw to his amazement that he was standing on the edge of another deep cliff. The forest appeared to go on and on because the trees growing up from below were even more gigantic than those around him. Their tops were even with the tops of the "shorter' trees growing around Mark. He peered downward as far as he dared but the canyon, if indeed it was such, appeared to be bottomless. He was in for an even greater shock when he returned to the place where the brook dropped over the edge. Some of the water had obviously been diverted into a crude catch basin around which small flower offerings had been placed! This meant intelligent life forms. A truly momentous discovery if he ever got back to base to claim it.

The light was going fast. He would have to fix a shelter of some kind. Not all the animals might be as friendly as the little creature he'd seen earlier. A musical trill which ended on a questioning note caught his attention as he explored a thicket of bushes for a safe hiding place. Before he could locate the source of the sound he was almost bowled over by a small furry body all arms and legs. It threw itself at him and clung to his neck with arms and firmly wound prehensile tail. In an instant he realized it was not an attack but fear which drove the creature into his arms.

Was this a lost pet fearful of being out alone at night? Might he hope the intelligent beings were quite enough like himself to represent safety to the shivering bundle of fur which clung so tenaciously to his neck?

What followed was almost like the old game of Hot and Cold that he had played as a child. If he walked in one direction, the poor thing would shiver and chitter fearfully. When he went in the right direction, his new found friend would stop shaking and croon. It soon was confident enough to point a spiky little finger toward the tree nearest the cliff. When Mark walked over to the side facing away from the edge, the animal scrambled up to teeter precariously on his head and reach high for a peg above his own small head.

There appeared to be a ladder there which started several feet above the ground. Obviously it must lead to some refuge, for his new found friend swung up and out of sight. Mark took out the perma flash he had avoided using because of attracting some unwanted attention in a strange place. Carefully screening the beam, he could make out a series of holes leading up the trunk. The natives probably carried a set of pegs to work their way up. He was searching desperately for something to use for such a peg when three landed near his foot. His new friend above had not forgotten the help his human ladder had given him.

Mark lost no time in using the pegs to work his way up. Placing one in a hole as far as he could stretch with his leg, he stepped up. Placing the next two, holding to one while standing on a second to reach down for the bottom peg and so on he worked his way carefully until he reached the first lofty branch. There he found his sleek little pal waiting anxiously. While he caught his breath the small creature chittered in soft tones and stroked his arm. Mark could barely make out a line of pegs leading upward. Perhaps there was more to discover higher up. His friend seemed to approve of this move and scampered on ahead. Mark found the three missing spaces and replaced the pegs he had used, in their proper spots. He might have to borrow them to get down in the morning. Another lengthy climb brought him to a small platform with an artfully woven dome forming a tiny refuge. Mark was just able to crawl in and lie down. Close but cozy quarters. As soon as he had settled down the little animal crept over and snuggled as close as it could, finally insinuating itself gently inside his jacket where it settled down to sleep after chirping softly.

A sense of not being alone brought Mark awake, but his training kept him from betraying that awareness. Slowly as though moving in his sleep he rolled over and let his arm fall across his face. The movement caused a sleepy chirrup from within his jacket and the warm spot against his chest moved as the animal resettled itself.

From under the shelter of his arm Mark cautiously opened his eyes keeping his breathing steady feigning sleep. Beyond the small curved doorway loomed the giant trunk of the tree. Seated on her haunches almost invisible because her skin color matched the red brown of the tree's shaggy bark, was a small dark-haired woman. Her delicate features accented by large dark eyes fixed so intently on the door of the hut.

Mark stretched slowly and smiled hoping to give the impression of peaceful intentions. At his first move a wicked needle-like dagger appeared in the hand of the now tense native. As he sat up his little friend popped up poking its head out of the collar of his jacket and extending its paw to pat his face happily. Mark scratched the little head and told his wee friend that everything was all right. He was surprised to see that the black fur reflected the daylight with brilliant flashes of red and green much like a hummingbird's feathers. This was a beautiful, intelligent lovable pet. Did it belong to the woman who now guarded the only way out of his sleeping quarters? He really must have startled her with his red hair and fair complexion.

When she saw the little animal appear the native chirruped an imitation of its call and held out the hand not encumbered with a weapon. It scampered toward her and then stopped, suddenly turning to dash back into Mark's arms. "BaBa" she called several times. Every time she called, BaBa would dash forward then back to Mark.

This could have gone on all day as BaBa teased her owner. "BaBa," Mark pointed to the animal. "Mark," he said pointing to himself.

Finally the girl pointed to herself. "Rica" she said slowly several times. Taking this as a sign of recognition Mark eased out of the hut and stood up.

"Go to Rica," he ordered the animal holding BaBa out at arm's length. BaBa refused with speedier twitters and a vigorous shaking of her head. She then strengthened her refusal by climbing onto his shoulder and clinging stubbornly to his neck. The only thing Mark could do was to laugh helplessly

"Stop it you stubborn imp, you're tickling my neck with that tail of yours." Rica watched in surprise at Mark's laughing struggles with BaBa. Then she moved aside and pointed down with her dagger. Mark eased past her and climbed down the peg ladder until he got to the branch closest to the ground. There he had to stop because he didn't have the pegs BaBa had thrown to him the night before. He wanted a chance to take a quick look at the scene below him too.

The trunk was ringed by a circle of Rica's people, the men holding spears. The mystery of where they had all come from was solved when Mark discovered the cleverly contrived bridge between the edge of the canyon and the enormous tree that was nearest the cliff side. It resembled a drawbridge and was probably drawn back at dusk or he would have noticed it last night. Perhaps BaBa had wandered too far to get back to the bridge before it was moved back the night before. Mark's appearing on the spot when the frightened animal needed help was a lucky accident for them both.

Beyond the men below, the women of the tribe were moving swiftly in the welcome sunlight, making fresh floral offerings at the small shrine and filling the waterskins to take back into the trees. Tree dwellers? Highly possible he thought. These massive giants have limbs large enough to serve as one lane roads for sports cars if level. The natives were all short, slim, dark-haired and the same red-brown as his captor. How frightening he must appear to them, tall, red-haired, blue-eyed and wearing strange clothing. Certainly BaBa, perched on his shoulder and draped over his head was familiar and obviously very much taken with Mark. He hoped they'd take that for a friendly omen. If he could make peaceful contact with them, his find would be an important one. The natives, if willing, could help them with their explorations.

While he had been watching the scene below, Rica had taken the pegs she wore on a belt at her waist and swiftly worked her way down to the ground. Now she was busily talking with a man who appeared to be the leader.

In the gloom the night before Mark had been unable to judge the distance to the ground from his perch on the limb lowest to the ground. He was now able to see that his coil of rope might be long enough to reach within dropping distance.

He didn't plan an escape but he didn't want to be kept above either. Working carefully out on the limb to the nearest offshoot which appeared strong enough to support his weight, he swiftly and expertly tied the line to the branch and slid to the ground. With a sharp jerk he retrieved the rope and turned to face the astounded natives who had pointed their spears in anything but a friendly manner straight at his chest. Baba chittered protectively and patted his cheek sympathetically all the while gazing at her former owner who stood just beyond the men.

Mark calmly coiled the slim lifeline and stowed it in its place on his survival belt. The men watched his every move. He smiled at them, patted Baba and spoke soothingly to the distressed little animal. Then he expressed his peaceful intentions in Basic knowing they probably didn't understand it at all. "No harm done in trying though," he thought ruefully.

He'd have to do something and soon. All the men had long, black carefully tended hair, most with braids and small ornaments of flowers or feathers. Perhaps he might show peacefulness in some way. His unruly hair had grown quite long since they had set out on the mission so he extracted the small steel comb he carried from its zippered pocket and tried to comb some order to his messy head. Now he had their attention and a few dropped to their haunches to watch warily. Mark pulled a thread from the lining of his jacket and held it in his teeth while trying to make a clumsy braid. Uh, uh, wouldn't work. So he fished out the small metal signal mirror, gave it to Baba to hold at arms length in front of him and tried again. The mirror was two sided keeping Baba fascinated with her own image thus holding it steady for Mark without realizing it. It was a tough job and a ragged one at that, but he finally had a small braid tied with a bit of thread. With the rest of the thread he tied the top of the braid as close to the scalp as he could. Then he sawed the braid off his head with his hunting knife. He hoped this would symbolize loss of strength and peaceful intentions. By now he had collected quite a crowd of onlookers both men and women. He wondered where the children were. Perhaps in their village for safekeeping.

His final gesture was an inspired one. Fashioning a small tube from the empty foil packet that had held his Sustain tablets, Mark put the end of the braid in and pinched the foil firmly around it. He offered it to the chief on his extended palm, smiling and bowing his head. There was a fearful moment of silence and a long wait before anyone moved. Finally the chief stepped forward hesitantly, stood on tiptoe, cautiously patted Mark on the head and accepted his offering. Suddenly the air was filled with chattering and the happy trills of Baba who sensed that all was well.

The chief had gone toward the shrine with his warriors following him. The women seemed to be waiting for Mark to follow before they joined the informal parade. Mark trailed after the chief at a respectful distance to watch him offer Mark's gift and set it down beside the tribe's flowers where the red hair shone just as brightly. Now everything seemed right for a pretty woman came forward and offered Mark a bark cup of water; another, some fruit on a leaf plate. He accepted both gratefully being both thirsty and famished. Baba impudently appropriated her share. She was lovely to watch with her sleek black head gleaming in jeweled color flashes as the iridescence was fired by the sun.

The oldest of the children had ventured across the bridge to stare at the stranger as he breakfasted. Seeing that the bold one was not harmed gave courage to all the rest and soon he was surrounded by laughing children eager to touch his head as he sat eating. These seemed to be a happy people of some intelligence. Mark was glad he'd found them. What roamed the forest at night to threaten them and force the use of tree refuges and a drawbridge? He didn't have to wonder long about one of the dangers they faced.

Attack!

★★★★

The peace of the sunny clearing was broken by a shrill shriek and the entire populace melted swiftly across the bridge including Baba. Mark was not quick enough to follow to the bridge which was quickly drawn out of sight. He stood in the middle of the clearing and searched rapidly for whatever it was that had uttered that terrifying cry. He was loath to leave the spot for sight was limited in the undergrowth which might offer safety as well as great danger.

Again the shrill cry and this time much louder. Only the appearance of a shadow gave him enough warning to drop and roll out of the way of screaming death on the wing. He was on his feet in an instant to face the giant winged lizard-like creature which had hoped to trap him in its cruel talons. There seemed to be very little chance of escape from the sharp beak at the end of a long, green, snakelike neck weaving so viciously back and forth. The creature was trying to hypnotize him into a daze. He scooped a handful of earth and threw it desperately toward those beady, glittering eyes, hoping to gain even a few seconds. His groping hand chanced upon the mirror Baba had been toying with and dropped in her panic-stricken flight to safety. Mark picked it up and flashed the bright sun's rays into that wicked face. Momentarily blinded the hissing dragon lizard drew back and Mark dashed toward the trees. At least there, the lizard would not be able to use its wings so easily and the fight might be a little more even. Several spears arched through the air and landed near his feet! The natives were trying to give him a chance with their small weapons. Mark snatched up several as he ran to the trunk of the nearest tree. The lizard followed flapping its giant wings so vigorously that small bushes were uprooted and dust swirled upward in miniature whirlwinds. It was plain to see that the creature would outlast his endurance in any prolonged fight. He would have to attack somehow.

With the massive trunk as a shield Mark kept dodging the lashing neck and the flailing wings, waiting for a chance to strike with a spear. He threatened the dodging head each time it appeared but after throwing a spear and seeing it bounce harmlessly off an instantly lowered leathery eyelid he knew he couldn't strike that vital spot. Then the lizard tried a curious maneuver that betrayed its considerable intelligence. Using its talons to grasp the tree trunk it balanced on its tail and tried to enfold Mark with its wings and pin him to the trunk. If Mark stepped back or tried to run to the next tree he would be caught by the powerful jaws at the end of that long neck. He put his back to the trunk, a spear in each hand, and moved around under the huge body. There was a small space because the tail held it a little away from the tree. Dropping one spear and grasping the other with both hands, he braced himself against the tree and drove upward with all his might into the lizard's body where the huge leg joined the powerful body. Grabbing the other spear he slashed at the wing on the opposite side. The wounded creature pulled away to get at the spear so annoyingly ground into its flesh. The few slashes Mark had made in its wing on the other side continued to tear as the wing flapped putting it more off balance. Swiftly Mark slipped his coil of rope from his belt and fashioned a lariat loop with practiced ease. His first throw fell short and he knew he would have to move in closer to snag the head of the enraged animal. He was growing very tired and would have to make his move before the lizard focused his full attention on Mark again.

The rope snaked up and out as the lizard raised its head to shriek defiantly. The noose slipped over the opened beak and back over its head to encircle the neck. Mark ran around the tree snubbing the shortening rope and hoping that it would be long and strong enough to strangle his opponent.

Now the struggles of the thrashing giant as it tried to break the hold of the rope cutting off its breath threatened Mark's safety. He had to dodge the giant wings, flailing talons and wildly swinging head while keeping the line taut. He didn't know if he could keep holding on. Already overstrained muscles were cramping with excruciating pain. Suddenly someone behind him was adding help to his struggles. He turned slightly and through the salty sweat nearly blinding him, he saw several natives grasping the end of the rope and hanging on. Others grabbed them to help steady the human chain. Once their ancient enemy seemed trapped, they had bravely returned to make sure of it. With this, the battle turned and it was soon over.

The men cut the huge talons off with a sharp spear and solemnly presented them to Mark. He took the claws from one foot but presented the other to the first native who had grabbed the rope behind him. He was amply repaid for his gesture by the awe and pride reflected on that strong brown face and suspected he'd made a friend for life.

The chief now made clear to Mark through sign language that they would have to hurry and dispose of the carcass and take shelter from the animal's mate who would surely come searching when he did not return.

Together they struggled to drag the massive corpse farther down along the canyon lip away from the clearing before shoving it over the ridge to crash heavily at the bottom. It took so long to get to the bottom that the canyon seemed endlessly deep. Mark was more impressed than ever with the size of the trees whose roots were somewhere below and their tops towering almost to the clouds above him.

Preceded by a proud chief, Mark was led across the span into a frenzied crowd of all ages waiting to greet him. The little people lined the limb roadways happily reaching out to touch him as he passed. Despite his fatigue the surprise of what lay before him brought his curiosity forth and he wouldn't have stopped to rest until forced.

Once across the drawbridge, which was immediately retracted, and through a screen of hanging branches he entered another world. These people clearly lived their entire lives in the trees. The extremely wide branches were literally roadways where everyone traveled with a sure grace. He doubted if anyone ever fell off and was soon traveling as easily as his hosts. Where it was necessary to go from one space to another and a convenient limb was missing, woven fiber swinging bridges had been cleverly constructed. Hanging gardens for food and flowers hung suspended in flat baskets wherever a small ray of sunshine was able to pierce through. Mark was later to find that more extensive gardens grew much higher up. Platforms built from limb to limb supported the comfortable dwellings nestled against the trunks. They were always placed near enlarged knotholes or crevices in the tree itself which were further hollowed out of the living bark to provide a refuge safe from attack.

The pleasant community high in the green and gold light of the forest had more than natives. There was a very large variety of plants and small animals as well as a host of birds thriving in this special forest world.

Part of every scant costume were the three climbing pegs suspended from a belt around the waist which enabled the owner to climb to safety when away from the community proper. Levels within the town itself were reached by means of ladders but even these could be drawn up against unwanted intrusion. Until he knew the location of each tree with the line of peg holes that promised safety, each community member had to stay within its boundaries.

Everyone had assigned tasks which they performed without complaint. All food brought in by the hunters and gardeners were shared equally. No one seemed to lack for the basic necessities. Mark learned to appreciate his rescuers very quickly and spent hours talking with the chief and his elders. He soon had a primitive vocabulary in their language and taught them Basic in return. They were as fascinated with the knowledge he had to share as he was with their complicated culture. Because he had slain the dragon lizard, Mark was honored as a great warrior. The flying reptile was a fearsome enemy, preying regularly on the little people as a food source for its nestlings. Escape if caught in the open was almost impossible. No one had killed one before. It's shrieking hunting call sent everyone to the shelter of the inner rooms of their tree homes. The lizards seldom attempted attack within the forest itself because maneuvering the giant wings through the dense branches was difficult, but they were sometimes driven to attempt it by hunger and poor hunting elsewhere. When this happened, the woven mats of the outer rooms could be torn away. The hapless victim was snatched off his own doorstep unless he was safe within the bole of the tree and the entry blocked against attack.

His polished metal mirror, which he had used to help delay the lizard, was an object of awe. Everyone wanted to see into it but were afraid to hold it until the now great warrior, Grush, tried it even before the chief did

33

himself. One by one, Mark explained each of the items on his survival belt though he was never able to explain how he had captured the sun in his perma torch. Nightly, around the small fires in the cooking pots, he explained over and over to the assembled natives, the things he had. He held each in turn and signed with his hands their uses if words failed him. Now they added "teller-of-tales" to his status of warrior and "tamer of animals" because he had instantly charmed Baba who refused to go back to Rica, her rightful owner.

Sometimes he drew diagrams with charcoal on the waterproof back of his jacket to explain ideas and later washed them off. His fishing line and hooks puzzled them. They couldn't understand the idea of fish not having been near a stream large enough to see any. Nor did they know where the waterfall went after it reached the bottom. There was a strong fear connected with whatever lay at the bottom of the trees. Mark would have to know more if he was to venture away from this pleasant life as he must eventually.

Before that day came however, he was to make two useful improvements for his friends. First he taught them how to make and use bows and arrows. Their spears were their only weapons and with snares, their only hunting tools. The hunters soon became adept at using the bow and it became the favored weapon for catching game. It also meant more of the bright feathers they so favored for ornaments.

Aside from defense, the other major concern was water. The tribe and the others he was to meet all had to maintain their communities near the edge of the canyon rim at places where water was available. Carrying the water to the villages from springs or small streams was a major activity for the women and often a dangerous one. Under

Mark's supervision, the natives constructed a crude aqueduct system of bark troughs. They led from the stream at the lip of the canyon wall across a narrow drawbridge, to a large, wooden storage barrel resting on a strengthened platform between two strong limbs. A guard was kept at the water bridge to raise it whenever the larger span was drawn back to safety. The natives were so pleased with the improved water supply that they soon added refinements of their own extending the troughs along the roadways into the village itself thus shortening the carrying distance to individual homes.

Mark had finally been able to explain a little of where he'd come from and there were more like him. The chief expressed astonishment at the sketches of the bare mountain, nor could he believe totally in a land beyond, devoid of trees. He did understand Mark's wish to rejoin his own tribe, but shook his head violently when Mark suggested descending to the bottom to follow the stream from the waterfall. "Great, great danger! Comints very bad tribe. Eat the flesh of enemies." Obviously there was another tribe, unlike theirs, who lived on the forest floor and practiced cannibalism. The Kaptas and the Comints were bitter enemies. This explained the taboo about going to the base of the trees.

"Skin pale like white wood grub." He gestured with the squirming captive he was about to roast on a twig before popping the delicacy into his mouth. " No hair on head, little eyes like this," the chief said squinting. " Can see in the dark better than Kaptas. Dig pits and hide them. Use secret snares to trap. Bad! You go other way my son. I give Grush to you to help, Baba to scout."

It was a most generous offer. Grush was considered the number one warrior of the tribe and Baba's kind was rare, only a few were pets in the village. The old chief had grown very fond of Mark and would rather he stay; but if he couldn't keep him, he at least hoped to persuade him to follow a less risky path.

In the end Mark followed the chief's persuasive reasoning. The thought of travelling in near darkness of the damp, moldy undergrowth on the ground was not as attractive as going along the base of the cliffs he had to admit. Despite his fears of the unknown, Grush was eager to go with Mark. It was doubtful if anyone or thing could have persuaded Baba to stay behind. Before he left, Mark gave the chief, for safekeeping, a slender plastic tube containing his carefully written notes on the tiny sheets of paper all archeo-techs carried for that very purpose. If any of the team did turn up, the information would be of great value.

A Long Way to Rejoin the Team

★★★★

This time, Mark was a little more prepared to tackle the unknown. Grush was more familiar with food and water sources; Baba could scout and retrieve. The tribe had prepared a supply of dried fruits, meat, and a kind of journey cake made from dried berries mixed with chopped nuts and carefully packed in a skin pack sack. In the special pouch swinging on Grush's belt were the herbs used as medicine by the tribe. Both carried a spear and the bow and arrows Mark had introduced.

After many good wishes and tearful farewells, they started back the way Mark thought he had come. Grush found the small signs of Mark's passage which helped to make the return to the mountain wall near the spot that had been his first night's camp. After a short search, they found the stone marker he had fashioned as a guide for possible rescuers. Mark added a small note from the scant supply of paper remaining in his jacket, giving directions to the tribe.

Now they turned to follow the cliff wall past the spot marking the ancient waterfall. Grush was wide-eyed at the sight of the mountain. His people had never ventured this far from their village. They traveled only from their trees to their water sources.

At first, Baba clung to Mark's shoulders as fearful as Grush at being so far from familiar territory, but gradually, her irrepressible spirit and curiosity got the better of her. She would skitter ahead chattering constantly, picking up bits of things that interested her and bringing them back to share. Sometimes she would dash up to those trees she could climb and scout from on high. Though she wasn't able to speak, the intelligent little creature could convey simple messages by gesture. Baba was best at keeping them supplied with water for she seemed to have as unerring instinct for finding it when they were most in need.

Baba could find water and she craved the drinking of it, but she would do anything to avoid getting the least bit wet. The few times it was necessary to ford small streams, she would cling precariously to the very top of Mark's head, her fingers twisting his hair painfully until they reached dry land where she would scamper off to the nearest tree scolding all the while.

Grush was a very different story, relishing the unaccustomed baths he soon learned to take whenever it was possible. The Kaptas were a very clean people but bathing as Mark did was unknown because of the tree dwellers limited supply of water. Tiny children were sometimes dunked in large pottery bowls for baths, but the rest made do with sparing splashes from a pitcher. When they chanced upon a small lake after several days of travel, Mark introduced Grush to two more wonders, swimming and fishing.

Up until now attempts at fishing in the streams they passed had proved fruitless. Mark had begun to think eatable water dwellers did not exist here and Grush thought fishing entertaining as a new kind of game though pointless. The lake looked promising so Mark was eager to try his luck again. He was not successful however until he fashioned a crude raft and tried nearer the center of the lake in deeper water. Here in fact, the fishing was excellent and he hauled in several tasty fish in very little time. Grush was amazed and wanted to try his luck too. Mark wisely decided to teach him how to swim before letting him on the raft. His forethought proved a wise move because the combined weight of both on the raft tipped it over soon after they had pushed off on Grush's first time afloat.

Grush proved a very apt pupil and learned to float after only one lesson. It took a little longer but he soon learned a very acceptable movement through the water even if it would never take a prize for correct form. After that, it was almost impossible to keep him from the water and Mark spent much time explaining the need for caution in strange waters.

The explorers spent several days near the lake much to Baba's distress. That much water was way too much for her, nor did she relish the taste of fish as well as her companions. However all good things must come to an end sometime and they finally decided it was time to continue their trek to find a way out of the valley.

The mountain chain they were following still remained the unclimbable barrier it had been but the forest at its edge began to change. It was not so dense nor the trees so tall. Little lakes and streams appeared more frequently. Gradually they seemed to be leaving the forest behind as small level meadows against the cliff face appeared. The mountains were gradually forcing them to go northwest giving Mark the impression that they were following the rim of a huge ring or bowl. At mid-day, the usual temperate climate was almost too hot as the sun was no longer kept from them by the cool depths of the forest they had left behind. Mark soon found it more comfortable to dress like a native. He had fashioned his jacket into a pack and adopted a woven reed loincloth Grush had made for him. Over this he wore his equipment belt to which he added three climbing pegs and the lizard claws. He was soon as brown as Grush having acquired an enviable tan which was accented by a mass of wild hair and a bushy red beard. Baba adored the beard, combing busy fingers through it whenever Mark would allow it, in an affectionate grooming ritual.

It was easy to become careless about their safety after days of unimpeded travel through seemingly friendly territory. No strange beasts were sighted to menace them, the weather had been great and only minor detours around natural formations had been necessary. They did take care to stay under the shelter of the trees and search the sky carefully for flying lizards before crossing in the open. Neither man wanted to meet one of those horrors again if they could avoid it.

Early one morning as they hiked toward the sound of roaring water which promised a very large river, Mark sighted smoke rising in the sky to their left, past a stand of trees downslope. Since they had no way of knowing whether it was due to a natural phenomena or to another tribe, they would have to scout.

Eagerly they pushed on to the riverbank only to discover a wide, swift current too risky to cross through the water. Unwisely they searched up and down the bank making no attempt at concealing their presence. They were so intent at finding a way across that they were not aware of being watched.

Mark finally decided to rig a rope and try to anchor it across the stream somehow and cross hand over hand. He knew he couldn't carry Baba on his head so he used the cloth belt from his jacket to fashion a harness for her. Baba was very happy with her new adornment, prancing and preening to show it off, never suspecting its real use.

They spent most of the day preparing the lines and Baba's harness, planning on crossing the next day. Mark explained to Grush that if either fell into danger the other was to escape as fast as possible and not try a rescue until success seemed possible.

"I'm sure that my people will follow me soon. If anything does happen to me, I want you to go back and wait for them so you can guide them to me. You will be able to give them much information about the dangers they face too."

Mark was right about his people. Without adequate supplies they had been unable to follow him after he fell. His signal rocket had reached the top of the cliff and seen by a very excited Scagen. The fact that Mark had survived the fall seemed a miracle to his best friend who vowed he'd be a member of the rescue party at all costs.

It took some time to work their way down the mountain to base where preparations were already underway for a rescue party. As soon as they were able to get clear signals through, Kayla had informed Terrell of Mark's mishap and probable survival. The rescue party would be larger than the original exploring team. Terrell decided to make the most of the forced opportunity to make a wider study of the unknown territory. The photographs taken at the summit had shown clearly the beauty and mystery of the forest below. It seemed to have the promise of several new life forms.

The problem of the communications barrier seemed insurmountable until Kayla suggested they send messages in several stages. They planned to reach the forest floor by bridging the gap to the nearest tree and using that tree to reach the ground. It was the same tree that had tempted Mark to lean out too far and which he had been unable to climb back up.

If the tree route proved possible then perhaps messages could be passed up and flashed by sight signals to a pilot observer or sent from a spot lower down the mountain. The task was simplified when they found that signals from the valley could be sent and received by an antenna projecting over the cliff's edge. Though radio signals were blocked by some mysterious quality of the mountain in that area messages could be sent by field phone through cables painstakingly stretched from the primitive shelter housing the newly established weather observatory. It perched on the sheltered side of the peak to a camp halfway down the mountain and from there radioed to base.

Even more remarkable was the ferry system used to lower the supplies the great distance to the ground below. All personnel crossed the precarious swinging rope bridge to the tree and then down the branches but supplies were lowered by a clever system of ropes anchored at the edge of the cliff.

Scagen was the first of the party to reach the ground. Eagerly he searched for signs of his lost friend. It wasn't long before he found the pile of stones containing Mark's message. It was read avidly by every member of the search party as each reached the ground. Word for word it was sent back to base where the information about the new tribe astounded the scientific teams. The warning of the flying lizards was carefully noted by the team at the weather station who did not wish to become the next item on a dragon menu.

As soon as all supplies were transported and camp set, the search party divided into two teams. Since transmission was not hindered in the valley itself, they could keep in touch. One group would follow Mark's trail to the village and make contact with the Kaptas, the other would follow Mark and Grush.

While Mark was making plans to cross the river, his friends were preparing for the next day when they would start in search of him.

Kayla was assigned to the village team while Scagen, who had argued for the assignment went with the team following Mark along the cliff side of the mountain. When Kayla's team reached the pool where Mark had his first drink, they were startled by a shadow slipping from the tree into their midst. Rica, frustrated because she couldn't go with Grush and Baba, had contented herself by keeping vigil near the spring for the people Mark was sure would come. The team language expert was pleased to hear the few words of Basic speech Rica had learned. This meant that establishing rapport was going to be fairly easy.

Rica led them gracefully through the fragrant green world to the clearing Mark had reached in wonder several weeks before. It was fortunate that Mark had left a message or the sight of his red hair decorating the forest shrine would have been more than a little unsettling.

The quick musical trill Rica used as a signal was answered by another and the rolling forth of the drawbridge. Before they had time to wonder at the cleverness of the construction, the chief and his warriors had crossed for a formal greeting after which he solemnly handed over the message Mark had left with him.

Mark had been an excellent ambassador for they were on a friendly basis with the tribe almost immediately. Touring the village and viewing the aqueduct system so proudly displayed by those who helped build it, was an interesting and rewarding experience. Kayla knew she

43

would enjoy her stay with the villagers as part of the anthropology research team.

As a pioneer trail blazer, Mark had done an equally good job. Scagen and the others had little difficulty following the trail he had so carefully blazed.

Careless Mistake

★★★★

Mark had become too complacent about his safety. He had prepared the others for disaster and then forgotten to plan for himself. The next morning all looked calm except the wild water rushing before him. After several casts with his rope, he succeeded in anchoring it around a boulder on the opposite side. Several hard tugs with the combined muscle power of Grush and himself satisfied Mark that the rope was secure enough to support his weight. He would go over first and then Grush would send over the pack with Baba as passenger before he came over himself.

Gingerly Mark suspended himself monkey fashion under the rope to work across hand over hand, dragging his feet draped over the strand. The roiling water was only inches from his back. It was hard work but he finally made it. Scrambling the few inches to the top of the bank, he swung his arms to relieve the cramping of his muscles and turned to look about. He had just a few seconds to yell at Grush before being captured. The last thing he saw was his friend slashing the rope and snatching up his pack and Baba before disappearing into the grove that had sheltered them the night before.

Mark stumbled along the trail, his hands bound painfully behind his back. His captors forced him to follow at a quick pace and to make sure he didn't lag, another walked behind him to prod him with a knobby club. Though he was a captive, it was clear to Mark that they were in awe of him for some reason. The few words he had heard his captors speak were impossible to translate as they seemed to be more a series of hisses than articulated words.

He didn't wonder at this for long after he had been able to study them more closely. By some trick of evolution, they seemed to be more snakelike than human. Their skin was rough, almost scaly and had a greenish cast to the dark brown color of it. The hairless heads lacked nose and eyelids though there were breathing slits where a nose would be and small round green eyes. That they could hear, he knew from their actions, but except for a slightly different patch of skin where ears might be, there were no visible ears. These creatures moving swiftly on short legs supporting bulky bodies must have some intelligence as their ambush proved. He wondered how long they had been watching them.

Another of their strange habits nearly cost Mark his life. When he was brought to their village, he was tied to a post in the center of a large dusty circle. Crude mud huts surrounded this central meeting place where he was tethered in the merciless sun. One man was left to guard him, not so much to prevent escape, but to keep the smaller members of this strange people from poking him with sticks or trying to take the items dangling from his belt. Mark needed water desperately, he could hear it running nearby but he couldn't make them understand the need. Looking about through the glare of sunlight and the sweat dripping in his eyes, Mark could see no evidence of cook fires or water pots. The inhabitants of the village were incredibly filthy. It occurred to him that they did not use water and would never give him any.

As the sun approached midheaven the young ones retreated to the shade of their mud homes. Even the guard napped in the shadow of the wall from the nearest hut. Mark had the nasty feeling that he'd come instantly awake at his slightest move. He sagged against the confining ropes of vine almost fainting from the exposure and the lack of water. Something landed on his shoulder and tried to force an object between his swollen lips. Mark opened his eyes and saw a large brown bird somewhat like a crow trying to offer him a big green fruit of some kind. He took the chance and like a nestling opened his mouth. The bird popped the globule in and flew off silently. Mark chewed the juicy fruit, grateful for the tangy liquid that refreshed his parched throat. He hoped that the crazy bird would return with another. It did several times, until the guard stretched and yawned, then his benefactor flew away out of sight.

The strange berries not only slaked his thirst but seemed to have restored his failing strength. He was able to withstand the heat and his tight bonds until evening. Then he was untied and thrust into one of the smelly mud huts. The door was closed by several thick logs moved into place by some of the males. A small space at the top allowed him to see a bit and admitted a welcome whiff of fresh air.

The same routine went on for the next two days with the bird bringing him berries whenever the guard nodded in the heat of midday. Mark soon realized that the creature was taking care not to be seen while this strange tribe took their midday siesta. Such caginess spoke either of considerable intelligence or careful training. Who or what might have trained the bird?

Mark had tried unsuccessfully to dig his way out of his miserable hut. The back wall was solid rock and the mud itself hardened as solid as any brick. He was puzzled at the way he was being held. The natives made no attempt to feed him or remove his equipment belt. In fact, the adults lack of curiosity about the things dangling from his belt was as strange as their disregard of water. He was obviously a prisoner but he had no idea why or when it would end. If it hadn't been for the bird's feedings and the few journey cakes he'd kept in his belt pouch, he would have perished after the second day of captivity.

Shortly after being tied to the post on the morning of the fourth day, Mark felt the bird fly to perch on the bindings which held his hands securely behind his back. Though he couldn't see what was going on Mark felt the beak rubbing along the tough thongs for a moment before he flew off. It had been a daring move unseen by his captors as they had gathered in an excited group before the door of the largest hut. From within came the sound of hissing chants and drum beats. Obviously some sort of ceremony was in progress.

As he slumped against the pole trying to conserve his energy Mark noticed a slight movement across the dusty ground. A small column of insects, almost ant-like in their one behind the other parade, were heading straight for his feet. Would he be eaten alive? As he watched, the nearly invisible column avoided his feet and climbed the pole. Out of the corner of his eye as he painfully twisted his neck to watch their progress, he could just see them as they crawled over his arm to his bindings. Mark couldn't see what was happening, but aside from the creepy feeling when they crawled along his arm for a short space there was no other sensation. He was relieved to think that they weren't after his flesh. The bird must have rubbed something on the thongs that attracted these particular insects. Would they weaken them enough for him to break free? He'd have to wait. It would be useless if he made a move too soon. His guard had returned reluctantly when the drumming started and now leaned in the shade staring at him ceaselessly.

Suddenly the drumming increased in intensity, the children squealed and squirmed quickly away from the doorway of the hut as a large figure burst from within.

This wildly painted and befeathered individual must be the chief or a powerful medicine man. He towered above the slightly reptilian natives seemingly not of their type. As this garish apparition danced and chanted around his pole, Mark realized with a shock that his feet were like his and not the webbed toes of his captors. He watched more carefully going over every detail slowly.

Surprising Discovery

* * * *

There! In the woven headdress was the crude representation of a spaceship and below that the hair, pulled through the tightly fitted cap supporting the colorful creation, was as red and curly as his own. He didn't understand what was going on but he felt more hopeful than he had in days.

Now the shaman was dancing closer and darting a little nearer to Mark as if daring him to challenge his authority. He began a weird chant and as he darted forward hurled a word of magic at Mark, "Dive! Dive!"

Mark straightened and smiled.

The next circling move brought "Center pool". All of this mixed with the hissing gibberish of the tribe.

Another darting move, "Signal"

It took time, but Mark gathered that he was to free his hands on a signal from the shaman and spit at him disdainfully.

What this would do he had no idea, but nothing had made much sense up to now anyway. He tended to trust someone more like himself than his captors anyway. Mark was in a very tough spot. He had to take a chance that this weird character prancing around him throwing in a few words of Basic was really trying to help instead of weaving some native spell.

Suddenly the dance ended with the medicine man standing right in front of Mark. The drums were silent, the villagers motionless in tense anticipation.

"Now" roared the shaman as he pulled his two fists apart and flung his arms wide to the sky.

Mark yanked hard at the thongs binding his crossed arms. They fell away easily and he stepped forward flinging his arms up in the same defiant gesture as the figure before him. Then he drew his shoulders up and spat disdainfully at the feet of the grinning man. Instantly a horrified protest arose from the villagers as they crowded forward menacingly, the men with lowered spears.

The shaman grumbled and cursed to show he had been insulted. Then he roared his sentence of doom upon the defiant captive.

Mark was herded in a circle of spears after the high priest who led the way to the edge of the village. From the frightened murmurs fading behind as they walked Mark guessed that they were being led to some sacred place feared by the villagers.

The sound of roaring water grew louder as they walked. The villagers feared water! That became even more clear as Mark watched the expressions on the faces of his guards as they bravely continued on their way behind the frightful figure ahead.

When they halted it was on the edge of a high bank facing a deep pool, fed by a branch of the river they had been following. On the opposite side in the solid rock of the mountain wall was a cave opening into which the waters of the pool poured to disappear in the bowels of the earth.

Mark stood there with the waving spears bristling at his back and gaped in wonder at the colorful symbols painted with Permalaq around the mouth of the cave. A planet with the symbol for Sularis' home planet, a crashed spaceship, and within the complicated meaningless designs around the lip of the opening, "survivors within". Incredible! Except for his precarious position the whole scene was almost laughable.

He did not have long to wonder about all of this before he was beckoned forward haughtily. The shaman gestured that he was to dive into the pool and swim through the opening. To the natives this meant sure death. The shaman ceremoniously removed his feathered bracelet and tossed it to the center of the pool were it floated on the rapid current over a drop into the cave entrance. It was a clever way to give Mark information about the current's direction.

"Now," the high priest hissed.

Mark took a deep breath and dove for the center of the pool. The cold water was breathtaking but a welcome refresher after his days in the sun and nights in the filth of the native hovel. He glided to the surface and swam as little as possible allowing the current to carry him along. He hoped that his head down position would convince the watching natives that he was nearly dead. The few swimming motions were meant to be death struggles.

The swiftly moving pull of the water falling into the cave swept Mark out and down into the utter dark of the opening. He had no way of knowing how deep the water was inside and braced himself for the shock of a painful landing. It was not nearly as bad as he expected. He came to the surface spluttering and unable to get a bearing in the dark. The cave opening glimmered faintly above his head.

Gradually he could make out the shape of the small cavern he was in. Treading water, he turned slowly wondering what to do until he saw a luminous arrow on the roof above him. He swam in that direction until another arrow brought him to a low opening. Mark ducked through and found he could stand in shallow water. Moving cautiously, with his hand on the wall to steady himself, Mark moved forward toward a pinpoint of flickering light.

Rounding a bend of the cool rock wall he was following, Mark saw a small fire flickering on a tiny sandy beach. Beside it rested a young Sularian woman about his own age.

"I've been waiting twenty years to meet another Sularian. Welcome," she said. "Come warm yourself by the fire."

Mark gratefully accepted the invitation and hauled himself on the beach to huddle near the flames. "How did you get here?" he asked. "I thought this territory was unexplored."

I was born here as was my brother whom you have already met."

"Born here!"

"Our parents were a part of one of the first survey teams sent out to explore Sularis twenty-five years ago. They were flying a small scout ship when they ran into a violent storm and crashed nearby. They avoided capture by the tribe who took you prisoner and managed to set themselves up as gods from the sky."

Karin promised to tell him more when they had reached the cave they used as a home. As soon as Mark

54

was warm enough, she picked up a flaming brand from the small fire and gave it to Mark taking another for herself. She carefully extinguished the fire in the sand, setting aside any unburned wood in a little stack for future use. Then she led Mark deeper into the mountain through several narrow passageways, climbing ever higher until they came into a large cavern where the light was bright enough to see without the torches.

"The hissers never venture this high in the mountains so we are quite safe here." She took him to the mouth of the cavern and pointed to her right. Dimly gleaming in the distance, Mark could see the crumpled fins of a scout ship.

"Our parents gradually salvaged every usable bit from the ship and carried it here. They set the rescue beacon and left the distort shield set to keep the natives away. The hissers as we call them, are not very bright. They have minimal intelligence level in fact. They are highly superstitious, have poor eyesight, and are very much creatures of habit. They may be dull mentally, but they are clever enough to be tenacious warriors so we never underrate them. If we have to move around when we might be seen, we do so during their siesta hours when they are in a torpid state. Their two biggest fears are water and fire. They don't use either of them.

"How can they exist without water?"

We aren't certain but guess that their scaly skin protects them from water loss. They might get necessary moisture from the foods they eat. They are mostly vegetarians though they will eat small animals and birds raw if they catch them. By the way, those claws hanging from your belt kept them at a respectful distance. That and your appearance. After all you don't harm gods, even strange ones, nor do you take possessions under the protection of the flying lizards claws. That ugly beast is their worst enemy and none of their warriors has ever killed one. How did you get them anyway?"

Just then Karin's brother Eril entered carrying the garish headdress he had worn when Mark first saw him. While he washed off the ceremonial paints and changed into a worn pair of uniform pants, Mark explained to his rescuers who he was, where he came from, and what he was doing there. Later, over a simple meal in the comfortable cavern, Karin and Eril took turns explaining how their parents had survived the crash for twenty two years, both dying within weeks of each other. They had never given up hope of rescue and had carefully taught their two children everything they could possibly recall. They were trapped in the valley by the curious communications blackout, the rugged mountain range, and the fear of the deep forest. Once in the three years before Eril was born, they had managed to elude the hissers and cross the river. They had ventured into the forest following the river that ran the length of the broad canyon floor. They hiked deeper into the musky, slimy atmosphere beneath the giant trees, until they met the Comints. They were sickened by the sight of those repulsive creatures feasting on some hapless animal. They escaped back along the river, followed by the Comints who were wary of them only because the Sularians were strange to them. It was necessary for Eril's father to stun two who came too close as they neared the safety of the sunnier spaces near the edge of the forest. They were revolted to see the Comints fall upon the still living bodies of their fallen comrades to devour them. Fear kept them from trying to get through that way again. If they had met the Kaptas, their lives might have taken a different turn.

"Where did that bird come from that fed me and saved my life?", Mark asked.

"Oh Caw," Eril laughed. "My sister has an interesting talent. Isolation from others has given her the time to develop her rapport with animals. Caw is a special pet of Karin's and I think the feeling is mutual. He is also an excellent sentry warning if the hissers get too close. You see, we do show ourselves for certain ceremonies our parents passed on to us. The hissers don't realize that we aren't the same gods who first appeared years ago when they fell from the sky and hatched from that crumpled egg half buried on the mountainside. We don't want them to locate our hidden home here so Caw keeps us informed."

"He also does simple tricks on command," Karin explained. "I used to feed him that way when he was a baby. I rescued him you see, and when he started feeding me back, I encouraged that habit. All I did was direct him to feed you instead of me."

"He seemed to avoid the hissers."

"Certainly! Caw values his tail feathers They are highly prized by the hissers."

"What did he do to the thongs tying my hands?"

"Rubbed a lump of animal fat on them to attract fat eating insects. Their saliva helped to weaken the thongs," Karin explained. "Come on I'll show you my private sun porch," Karin urged.

"Be prepared for quite a hike," Eril warned. "It's the other side of the mountain."

Karin explained the system of fluorescent markings her parents had used to mark their explorations of the many passages honeycombing the mountain as they walked. They had carefully used the supplies they had salvaged from the scout ship to keep from getting lost. Later they guided the children until they grew familiar with every passage.

Mark found Eril's warning to be very real as he toiled behind Karin up a steep passage that eventually led to an opening onto a wide ledge overlooking the wastes below. The ocean glimmered as a silver sliver on the horizon.

"Why didn't your parents try to escape this way?" asked Mark.

"Neither were experienced mountain climbers and they felt it too risky. Besides without proper supplies they couldn't exist long in the wasteland. There is plenty of water in the valley but we can't find the outlet that leads to the ocean. The stream leading into our caves does disappear eventually into a large cavern that is an underground lake. We don't know where or how it drains out."

"If your Dad had been able to climb down a ways and try his communicator, it might have worked. We found we could use ours until we reached a certain altitude on our climb."

"I don't think it occurred to him that there was any problem with reception. He was convinced the fault lay in the equipment itself."

"If he gave up using it because it was faulty, the power pack might still work. With your help I could try climbing down for a try at sending a message. If I reach base, we stand a chance of rescue."

It was too late in the day to try a descent and equipment had to be readied. They returned to the cave to explain to Eril what Mark wanted to do. There they found a very agitated Caw trying to draw Eril's attention to something urgent. Karin grabbed her father's distance lenses and trained them on a commotion on the other side of the village.

"The hissers have made another capture and are bringing him to the village."

Mark grabbed the lenses and focused them on the triumphant band of warriors. "Grush. They've captured Grush and Baba too. I told him not to try to rescue me but to go back and try to contact my people when they came. What will they do with him?"

A Plan of Action

★★★★

"Who is Grush? Baba?" Eril asked.

"My Kapta guide and friend. Baba is a charming creature who adopted me. The Kaptas call them "rare friend" but they are rather like the long-haired monkeys of Earth. Baba wasn't with me when I was captured because she hates water and had to be forced to cross the river. Grush must have followed the river to an easier crossing."

"We'll have to rescue them somehow, Eril!" Karin pleaded.

"Saving your friend Grush may be a little easier than rescuing your pet. Depends on how hungry the hissers are. That colorful pelt alone is an attraction."

"Oh, Eril don't say that!" cried Karin.

They watched from above as Grush was tied to the same post where Mark had been held prisoner earlier. Baba had been allowed to scramble up to cling fearfully to the top of Grush's head while a group of warriors argued over her fate and ownership.

Karin paced restlessly while the men discussed how to rescue the captives. "The rock eagle! I'm going to see if it can be of help." She explained to Mark that she had saved an injured rock eagle chick and raised it almost to maturity before it flew off to find a mate. "Sometimes he'll come when I call and do the few tricks I taught him just to please me. He's highly intelligent but very independent."

Moving carefully so she wouldn't be seen, Karin crept down to an exposed flat rock and crouched behind the boulders forming a half circle around the outermost edge. She cupped her hands and uttered the piercing whistle which was the eagle's hunting call. For long moments nothing happened and then her call was answered.

A very large bird with an equally impressive wing span spiraled gracefully down to land in front of Karin, his mottled grey feathers making him almost invisible against the rocks behind him.

Before he could utter his praise of the bird's magnificent appearance, Mark was hushed by Eril's hand over his mouth signing silence.

Karin was scribbling a crude sketch of Baba perched atop the pole where the animal had retreated temporarily out of reach of the short arms of the hissers reaching for her. The eagle followed every line as Karin scratched in the scanty layer of dust with her knife. He seemed to grasp the idea and Karin's soft command to "Fetch". He soared into the air and flew directly toward the squabbling group of natives below. Before reaching them, he uttered a challenging scream and dove straight for the terrified Baba who had no place to go. All in one magnificent sweep, he swooped down scattering the frightened natives in his path, grasped the harness around Baba's back with his strong talons, jerked her from the post, and swept back into the air. He carried the frantically struggling animal swiftly back to the rocky niche where Karin waited to catch his burden as he dropped it. Baba flung her furry arms around Karin's neck so tightly she almost strangled the girl who was trying to hand the eagle a favorite snack as his reward.

Mark, seeing the difficulty, whistled softly and
Baba delirious with joy and chittering a loud greeting
scrambled to find her beloved master. Her regal rescuer,
busy wolfing his reward paid no attention to her going. He
allowed Karin to give him a good scratching around and
under his neck feathers. Then took to the air again, diving
and swooping over the terrified natives below as though he
enjoyed a new game, before flying out of sight.

The hissers might have poor eyesight but Grush did
not and he had watched the rescue aware that the eagle was
not on a killing hunt. He had recognized the familiar
chitter Baba used when greeting Mark as it drifted back
barely within his keen hearing at that distance. It gave him
some comfort to think that though he had been unable to
rescue his friend, his friend might be able to save him.

To say that Baba was overjoyed to be with Mark
again would be an incredible understatement. She crooned
and patted his face, hugged and tugged and ran circles
around his legs. She climbed him like a tree to peer into his
face and chitter unanswerable questions in such an amusing
pantomime that Karin and Eril were soon in hysterics.

Finally exhausted, they all collapsed on the sleeping
furs to pull themselves together before they continued
planning Grush's rescue. Baba allowed introductions to
Eril and Karin but she wouldn't leave the shelter of Mark's
lap, eventually falling into an exhausted sleep as they
talked.

"They won't do anything with him before tomorrow
except to throw him in the hut as they did to you. They
probably believe him to be your servant because of the
lizard talons on his belt much like yours. For a warrior, a
god's servant, they will plan a warrior's death before they
sacrifice him to the pool. I think we can save him before he

dies but he'll have to put up with some rough handling before then. I was able to convince them that as a warrior you should be sent into the pool alive to meet your fate. You see you came here to fight me for the favors of the goddess." Eril sketched a courtly bow in Karin's direction, with a grin.

"If there is a search party looking for you, we'll have to work fast to prevent their falling into an ambush. The hissers are late sleepers because they seem to fall into a stupor when it's cold. They wait until the sun is well up before they start stirring about. As soon as it's light, I'll help carry any equipment you need to Karin's sun porch and do what I can to set it up. I hope you two can manage after that. I'll have to appear to the hissers to set things up for Grush. Karin, we'll need all the rest we can get. Can you fix a quick meal while we get supplies together? Fix a sun potion too." Eril explained to Mark that the sun potion was a blend of mountain herbs brewed into a tea. They used it to prevent sunburn and quench thirst when used before a long exposure. Eril would try to give some to Grush during the ceremonies tomorrow.

The sky was scarcely grey before Eril shook Mark awake. Karin had had the good sense to prepare breakfast while getting supper the night before to avoid wasting time in the morning. They ate quickly, speaking only when necessary. Mark tied a short line to Baba's harness and anchored it securely to prevent her following them and getting into mischief. Karin set a dish of food within easy reach should Baba wake before they returned. The poor thing was still deep in exhausted sleep when they shouldered the climbing equipment and left the cavern.

By the time they had trudged upward through the dark passageways, the sun had climbed high enough in the morning sky to give them ample light to rig the safety lines securely. Eril stayed only long enough to see that all was ready before he left to get into his witch doctor's disguise, as he called it. Mark wondered if Grush would recognize Eril as a friendly spirit. It would be necessary for him to, if he was to aid in his own rescue.

Mark strapped the communicator to his chest, checked the safety lines again and began a cautious descent. He was thankful for the tough skin boots the Kaptas had fashioned for him. They still fit after the dunking in the pool.

Karin watched fearfully from above wondering what she really would do if Mark fell. She understood now why her inexperienced parents had not tried this way as she watched Mark's snail-like progress down the rocky mountainside.

"Hope this isn't a useless risk of my neck", thought Mark as he carefully worked his way down to the point where he was at the end of the line they had to use. He was barely able to reach a shallow niche where he braced himself with his back to the rock and looked out to the dizzying view below him.

"Enough of that--better concentrate on what I came for." Luckily Karin had told him what little she knew about the use of the ancient communicator. In some ways it differed little from the newer, lightweight models that were so compact, making them much easier to carry. He should have no trouble in using it if only the power packs were still working. He flipped the switch to open and was rewarded with static, at least a sign of some power! Pressing the send button he gave his ident-call several times and waited. No answer. Mark kept trying. He didn't know how long he could stay before the chilling winds in his exposed position forced his retreat. If he waited too long he might get too cold to manage the demanding climb back. Just as he was about to give up hope he heard a faint call. Frantically he tried to adjust the unfamiliar dials he had been afraid to touch. He operated only the main ones he was sure of, for fear of upsetting the previous adjustments made by Karin's father.

"Mark, come in Mark!" Terrell's normally calm voice was strained with excitement as it suddenly boomed from the communicator. "Give the call letters on your equipment. Mark can you hear me?"

"Mark here. Perched on unknown mountain. ES 237"

"Impossible!"

"This impossibility is breathing." Tersely Mark gave him the information about his position and a little of what he had found, the Sularian survivors and a warning about the hissers.

"Rescue party with Kaptas. Search party on your trail. Found your pack at lake with pictograph message in charcoal on rock left by native guide. Have radio fix on your position. Communicators work inside valley. Try to contact party on other side of river. Will do same. Good luck."

"Mark, over and out."

The good news made Mark's wearying climb back to Karin's ledge seem a little shorter. She could see by the grin on his face as he climbed over the last ridge that he had been successful but she couldn't resist asking anxiously, "Any luck?"

"Lots of it! Let's get back and see how Eril's done."

They had one more thing to do before they left the sun porch. While Mark braced her from falling Karin reached as high as she could and painted her father's call letters in large colorful splotches to mark the opening of the cave passage as Terrell had instructed during their transmission.

Eril hurried back along the dark passageway to the cavern where he stopped only long enough to slip into the rough loin cloth, fancy feathered bracelets on ankles and wrists and the looped belts that were the basic parts of his God uniform. Before he picked up the headdress and a small drum he daubed on the colorful designs that concealed his features, with practiced speed. He and Karin had made the body paints from mud, animal fat and native coloring materials.

Then he slipped noiselessly into a small tunnel that led downward to a damp passageway emerging behind a thick pile of bushes screening the entrance. A small stream emptying into the sacred pool was an effective barrier to discovery by the water-fearing hissers. He glided into place before the bush and began a low rhythmic drumming. After a short space he howled to the sky and stamped his feet. Ah, that did it. On the path leading up the slope toward the pool the hissers were gathering, not daring to come too close to the water or to him.

Eril walked through the small stream slowly, making blessing signs to the water spirits before he stalked down the path proudly staring straight ahead. By this time the hissers had tied Grush to the prisoner post in the square.

"What are you doing with the manservant of my enemy?" he demanded hissing at the clan chief.

"Oh mighty one we captured him as a gift for you."

"Ah," he posed majestically. "I will prepare a fitting end for him so his soul will serve me instead of his master. Summon my drummers quickly!" Eril gestured impatiently.

Soon several tribal musicians appeared to tap out the magic music their god had ordered. While the hissers stood by in wide-eyed fascination, Eril began to bob and weave around the pole in much the same fashion as he had approached Mark.

As he chanted a string of senseless gibberish he wove in the message "Mark safe, help you". He repeated it several times and then said "nod head".

Grush had been frightened at first by this fearsome apparition. His tribe had its own gods and it was wise to respect those of others no matter how different they were. Besides he'd never seen a real one before. As the dance went on and he was able to study the dancer more closely he realized that Eril in disguise might be one of Mark's people. When he heard the few words in Basic, he relaxed a bit. Someone was on his side.

He was not so sure for long because suddenly the god came forward and ordered him to drink a most bitter liquid. As he choked and spluttered the god said a mumbled spell ending with "protect from the sun" woven in the jumble of meaningless sounds.

Then Eril ordered the warriors to sacrifice the prisoner to the guardians of the hot days and cold nights. Grush was untied from the post, pushed roughly along before two dangerously pointed spears and forced to walk the path toward the pool.

To one side of the path was a huge slab of rock slanted at an angle facing the afternoon sun. It fell away steeply on its backside facing the pool where there was a very narrow ledge before a drop into the water below. It was obviously a place of sacrifice as the stains upon the surface of the rock showed. There were four widely spaced stakes driven solidly into cracks in the rock. The god led Grush to the rock and pushed him flat. "Wait night," he mumbled as he gave him a shove. Quickly the hisser warriors strapped Grush flat in a spread-eagle position using the stakes to anchor the thongs tying his arms and legs. After more drumming and mumbo jumbo from Eril, Grush was left alone in the hot sun.

Grush was more fortunate than Mark though he didn't know it. Eril had been able to prevent some of the discomfort with the herb tea and he was lying flat rather than standing tied to a post. Nevertheless, he had to spend many agonizing hours alone in the hot sun. If it had not been for the special herb tea, Grush, despite his dark skin would have been badly sunburned in a very short time.

At midday while his guard nodded under a tree at the bottom of the slope Karin sent Caw to force some of the green berries into Grush's mouth. He didn't resist for very long, finding the fruit refreshing. Nor did he wonder at the strange way in which the food was delivered. So much had happened to him thus far that he ceased to find anything strange. Karin managed to enlist the aid of some more of her animal friends. This time, she sent the small grey rodents she kept as housekeeping pets in the cave, to gnaw quietly on the thongs holding the captive's limbs in place. She directed the animal's efforts from her precarious perch on the narrow ledge out of sight below the rock. In order to reach that spot, she had had to swim quietly around the edge of the pool with a basket holding her helpers balanced on her head, while being careful to avoid detection by the hissers. All this had to be done while the village napped in the heat as it was the safest time to avoid them. "Wait", she cautioned Grush with a low whisper and took her pets back along the way she had come.

After his siesta, the village chief came with his followers to view the captive from the bottom of the path well away from the threat of water. Satisfied that all was well, he returned to the business of his household. The hours dragged on.

Waiting too, were Eril, Karin and Mark. Just before sunset, they were to try the hardest part of the plan to save Grush. Mark, painted like a savage and carrying two unlit torches, eased his way carefully down the slope above the village to a spot behind some boulders several feet above the huts. There he waited.

Karin returned her pets to the cave and with Eril went to wait in the brush near to the narrow tunnel opening.

When the daylight was nearly gone and the hissers drifted toward their huts for the night, Mark made his move. Using his scout everlite he set the torches ablaze, leaped to the rock and started chanting "Old Man River" for lack of any other inspiration at the moment. He punctuated the lyrics with wild swings and stabs at the air with the flaming brands. The villagers cowered awestruck, all eyes in his direction. Even the guard stumbled down the path to stare. As soon as Mark had attracted the hissers attention, Eril and Karin, who had moved to the narrow ledge behind Grush, reached up and grabbed his pinioned arms. They struggled to drag him up and off the rock platform. The gnawed thongs broke loose with the tugging and they were able to pull the weakened native free, slip him into the pool, supporting him as they swam with the current into the cave.

Mark reached the end of his off key singing with an Indian war whoop. He swung the torches over his head and let them fly into the dust of the square where they would sputter out harmlessly. He dropped from sight immediately, moving as fast as he could in the dusk to reach safety. The hissers with the same thought in mind, headed in a panic for their huts.

Reunion

★★★★

Between them Eril and Karin were able to support Grush enough to carry him through the water to the sandy beach deep inside the cave. The struggle seemed endless but they finally staggered out of the water dragging Grush as far out of the water as they could. Grush was unconscious from shock and they'd have to revive him to get him to the safety of their cavern. It would be nearly impossible to carry him through the narrow twists and turns and up steep grades.

Eril started a small fire as Karin rubbed Grush's wrists and ankles to bring back his circulation. The gnawed thongs had eased his discomfort some, but the intense sunlight concentrated on the flat surface of the rock had finally made him lose consciousness. If Eril had not given him the herb potion and Caw the forced fruit, they might not have had time to save him. When the hissers found no trace of the captive in the morning, they hoped the natives would believe that Mark had claimed his servant, causing him to vanish.

Grush moaned and opened his eyes to stare at the two hovering over him. The gloom and the flickering firelight made their shadows into ghostly shapes on the wall. Seeing that the Kapta was badly frightened and disoriented, Karin hastened to tell him that they were friends that Mark and Baba were safe. Eril helped him to sit up and move closer to the warmth of the tiny fire.

Sorry to have put you through all that agony but we couldn't rescue you outright. We had to set the scene and make your disappearance seem mysterious to the villagers," explained Eril. Grush was not able to understand all of it, but he realized he was safe with friends.

As soon as he could stand with Eril's help they stifled the fire and started for the cavern. Eril led the way with Grush and Karin behind to help when she could. They had to stop several times to let Grush rest but they finally made it. They wrapped the shivering man in some sleeping furs and propped him up against the wall near to the tethered Baba. She was delighted to welcome her second-best friend with her joyous jumping act.

Karin busied herself with getting a late supper while Eril went to check on Mark. The village below was settled for the night, though uneasily for the torches still spluttered feebly in the square before the huts. Eril waited for his eyes to adjust to the gloom before starting off to look for Mark. He supposed that soon they would be leaving the valley that had been their home since birth. It would seem very strange and wonderful but very sad too. Harder yet for Karin who would have to leave her pets behind. As if called, Caw glided out of the darkening sky and landed on Eril's shoulder, rubbing his beak against the Sularian's ear in greeting, before he hopped off into the cave to settle for the night.

Suddenly Mark appeared with a happy grin spreading across his face, carrying the communicator. "Help is on the way. If we can get across the river the rescue team will be waiting. They don't want to disturb the hissers if we can get away without help, but they'll come if we need them."

"Tonight would be the best time while the hissers are still in shock over our little charade, but we should stay one more day to let Grush rest."

"Let's see what Karin thinks and have a look at Grush. He's pretty tough," suggested Mark.

If Grush had been feeling better he might have imitated some of Baba's antics to show his happiness at seeing Mark again, but he was too comfortable to move. He had been staring in wide-eyed wonder at the cave and its contents. It may have been simple almost primitive to Mark, comfortable to the Sularians who knew no other, but it was luxury to Grush. The cave had been furnished at first with all that could be salvaged from the scout ship and later with the necessities fashioned from native materials. It was a blend of technology and stone age cultures. He would not have the opportunity to examine it for long.

While they ate supper, it was decided that tonight really would be the best time to try to leave. Grush was to rest until the last minute. Eril and Karin had to sift quickly through a lifetime of belongings and decide what they could take. Caw watched the goings on nervously sensing something very different was taking place. All the things to be left behind were packed neatly into a small side cave and the entrance hidden with a large boulder pushed in place. Eril had set aside his feathered bracelets and spear; Karin some clay utensils and other oddments. These, with a basket of food they would be unable to carry, were to be left on the flat rock as an offering from their gods to the hissers. Mark and Eril slipped down to leave the gifts while Karin finished making up the packs. Grush had indicated that he felt well enough to help so he was to carry some of the food supplies.

Eril made sure to include his father's Survey logs and maps. Karin took the few small personal items that had been her mother's. She refused to leave her little pets behind so they were strapped in a small woven basket to the top of her pack. If Caw would follow, she wanted him to come too.

Mark was in charge of the communicator. Because he had lost his pack, he could take some of the things that the others might have had to leave behind. By the time they had finished, they had less than four hours to slip past the village and reach the riverbank. Once they were well out of earshot, Mark would try to make contact with the team. They would need help in getting across the water. Here Grush might be of help. He might be able to show where he had crossed.

They worked their way through the stone passageways to the opening behind the bushes and passed carefully one by one through the opening. Caw refused to follow them into those dark ways and Karin could only hope that he would come to her call once they were on the trail in the open. It was difficult to work their way in the darkness over the rocky shoulders bordering the pool to the narrow ledge below the rock platform. They finally had to chance a small light from the perma torch on Mark's belt. Easing along the narrow ledge with cumbersome packs without falling into the water was the worst of all.

It took more time than they had expected, but they finally won their way to the small grove of trees on the far side of the village. Instead of going straight through on the hisser trail to the river bluff where Mark had been captured, they skirted the edge of the grove and headed at an angle to reach the river farther on. Twice Karin halted to risk calling Caw but sadly her friend failed to appear. She knew he was capable of surviving on his own but she hated to leave him.

Mark had not leashed Baba once they were out in the open. She was content to ride in the cozy spot provided by his shoulder, neck, and the rise of the pack on his back with her tail coiled lightly around his neck.

Eril and Karin, used to the darkness of the caverns, found it easier going in the night-shrouded woodlands than the other two. They would have to wait until first light before any crossing of the river could be attempted once they reached it. In the meantime, they hoped to put as much distance as possible between them and the hissers. The wonder of the gifts they left behind might deter pursuit for a while, but if a keen-nosed hisser happened onto their scent, they might be hunted down. They would fight only if they must save themselves in no other way. Survey regulations prohibited upsetting any native culture unless it was unavoidable.

The roaring of the river in its swift passage was now getting louder, a welcome sound, telling them they were at least traveling in the right direction. Mark stumbled into a small brook flowing toward the larger watercourse. Remembering an old Indian trick to avoid pursuit, he urged his companions to walk in the chilling stream for a short distance hoping to end their scent trail. "A good idea, Mark, " Eril commented. "The water will stop them anyway as they fear it greatly. It will take them some time to go around though it may mean attack from an unexpected direction."

They waded along the small rivulet until they could stand the cold no longer, before scrambling out onto the opposite bank. Grush had struggled manfully on, but he was visibly tired, reaching the end of his strength after the ordeal of the past days. Mark and Eril hung his pack on a stick between them, while Karin supported the exhausted native until they could stagger on for a distance away from the brook. It would be necessary to rest, but they wanted to be out of sight and as close to the river as possible before stopping.

"Our hissers are not the only ones to fear," Karin said. "Dad told us that he thought there might be other clans in the territory. That's one of the reasons we have not explored too far away from our tribe's known range. We'll have to be doubly careful now. I haven't been this far before. Have you Eril?"

"No, at least not upstream. I've gone a bit farther downstream, close to the beginning of the mighty gorge. Some miles from here, the river becomes a boiling cataract before it drops over in a tremendous waterfall. I can't even guess at the distance to the bottom of the canyon below."

When they could push on no farther, they crawled into the center of a brushy patch of vegetation that offered scant protection and settled wearily against their packs. Karin gave each a small portion of the food they carried and sips of herb tea from her flask. Her wee pets, night creatures by habit were busily chittering around their small cage so she included them in the snacking. She tried again to call Caw but received no answer. Mark had better luck with the communicator. Scagen was on watch with the rescue party and by luck was monitoring when Mark's call came through. The rescue party was already at the riverbank awaiting them and had scouts at intervals to spot them wherever they emerged from the forest on the opposite bank. They were trying to get a fix on the groups's position with the com signals. "Avoid the area to the north of you. Animal activity of unknown nature there. Good luck!"

Taking turns at watch and sleeping fitfully passed the time till dawn slowly. All were barely rested when Eril awoke them and urged them on. When they pushed out of their hiding place, they saw how wise they had been to stop when they did. Here the ground before them gave way to a gentle brush dotted slope ending in a very large meadow before them. In the distance, they could see the gigantic trees of the Kaptas territory. In the slightly cup-like center of the grassland there was the now familiar group of huts built by hissers. It was the same even to the prisoner post in the center of the square except that this village didn't rest against the protection of a mountainside.

They would have to work their way around the ridge to the fringe of trees beyond. This time they wouldn't have any water to hide their tracks nor any gifts to delay pursuit. Besides, the Sularian's carefully developed witch doctor fiction was unknown to this tribe and couldn't be used.

The short rest seemed to have benefited Grush more than the others. He was able to carry his burden and keep up with the stiff pace Eril set through the tearing weeds and brambles at the meadow's edge. Speed was necessary if they were to reach the shelter of the trees before the rising sun warmed the villagers. Eril wove a zigzag course to take advantage of the little concealment offered by every bush and brush patch until they were able to reach the first small trees. All of them increased their speed to struggle out of sight and seek the welcome shade after the growing heat and the weight of the packs threatened to melt them. An added incentive was the small sounds signaling that the hissers were awake.

Despite the danger, Karin risked calling Caw one more time only to be disappointed again at no response from her beloved companion. Sadly she turned and followed the others now moving at a punishing pace toward the river.

A shining glint of moving water in the sunlight signaled their goal was near before they finally came to a high bluff overlooking safety on the other side. "If we can get a line across the water here we'd be safer I think, Eril said. See farther up the trees thin out and we'd be more exposed."

Grush signaled that up stream, a day's travel, they would be able to ford the river.

"Do we dare risk another day on this side of the river? If the hissers back there get wind of us they'll be on our tails for sure," Mark objected.

While they were debating their course of action the sharp eyes of Grush spotted something on the opposite bank, Mark following his lead saw a Sularian scout working his way cautiously upriver. Mark stepped from concealment and risked a short hail and was immediately answered. Now he could see there were several others with the advance scout. He melted back into the brush where they were hiding and risked the use of the communicator.

Soon a strong line snaked across above the river, caught expertly by Grush and handed to Baba who scampered with it up to a large branch of a sturdy young tree. Under Mark's direction, she looped it around the branch several times and brought the end to him. He used it to climb up and complete the knots to secure it. Now they had the means to begin transport. One of their lines was tied to Baba's harness and she was coaxed into swinging across the river on the first line trailing theirs behind. Though she hated to leave Mark, she seemed to sense the urgency of the situation and after much soulful chittering and face patting, she took off hand over hand, swaying above the rushing water until she was grabbed firmly by the nearest scout on the other side. Now the pulley system began and the first thing sent back to the fleeing party was a pair of stunners. The packs were transported easily and the bosun's chair rigged under Baba's anxious eyes.

Karin was the first across that swinging rope link to safety. She was midway across the river when a screaming rock eagle hurtled out of the blue above and attacked something in the brush near the river. Alerted, Mark swung the stunner in that direction just in time to halt the charge of a hisser.

"They're on to us," he shouted to Eril. "Fall back to the tree and I'll keep you covered."

Another diving charge and sweep upward by a dark flurry of feathers pointed the way for Mark to spray another enemy creeping from the other side. Caw working with the eagle was doing his best to help them escape. Mark had to be careful not to gun down their feathered helpers as he picked off the hissers pressing their attack.

Eril helped the protesting Grush into the sling and forced him across to the safety of the other shore. The hissers puzzled by the fall of their companions without any visible injury slowed their charge long enough for Eril to get across the river.

Mark was the last to flee aided by the distractions provided by the eagle and Caw. He managed to slip into the sling and escape in a rain of spears. One of the braver hissers tried to cut the rope lashed out of reach of his short arms, by sawing at it with his spear. The tough strands held until Mark reached the farther shore to be engulfed in a crushing bear hug from Scagen.

Caw landed squawking, to strut proudly up to a delighted Karin, demanding his reward for saving them all, while the rock eagle swooping in graceful circles called good-by before wheeling off to his mountain.

After gathering in the rest of the rescue party, the team hiked back to the camp at the lake Mark had discovered earlier. Here they remained several days resting, reporting and getting acquainted with each other's adventures.

Grush had initially obeyed Mark's orders to look for his people but when he reached the lake, he could not go any further. He just could not abandon the friend who meant so much to him, so he left Mark's pack and the crudely drawn message. It was discovered as he hoped it would be and his message clear enough to give the rescue team warning of possible dangers, the river and the hissers.

Eril and Karin were the objects of much interest as were the detailed logs his father had kept after the crash. Most of those in the party were only children or not yet born when Eril and Mara Escart were sent on their ill-fated scout mission. They were assumed dead after five years and no idea of their survival and family was ever considered.

Terrell was anxious to meet the two young castaways as he had been a close friend of their parents. He would have to wait impatiently for their return to base camp. This is what the party now set out to do, but first they were to return Grush to his people and collect the rest of their teammates.

Several days of easy walking brought them to the trail leading to the village spring. Kayla and Rica were waiting to greet them and lead them to the feast set up for their welcome. The Kaptas were proud of Grush and wanted to hear of his adventures. No one of their tribe had ever ventured so far from the home trees. Baba went into the hysterically funny gyrations signaling her joy at being back but despite her elation, she made it clear that she would not leave Mark.

Baba's obvious determined devotion caused a diplomatic problem. It was government policy not to take anything of value other than scientific specimens or gifts from native peoples. Wherever they went, the teams were to make as little impact as possible. Baba would have to be made to stay behind when they left.

The chief finally solved the problem by formally giving Baba as a gift of appreciation for bringing new friends to the tribe and great honor to Grush.

Eril and Karin were as enchanted with the gentle Kaptas as the others were. Despite the sophisticated knowledge passed on to them by their parents, they were almost more akin to these people than to their own in their feelings and real knowledge of the world outside.

The teams stayed several days before starting the climb back to the top of the mountain range. They would leave behind two members of their group to act as liaison between the valley and the outside world. When it became clear that Mark would not be staying, Grush volunteered to go with him. "I will learn for my people what is beyond the mountains," he stated firmly.

"Rica goes too. I am Kayla's friend," the Kapta girl asserted.

The two Kaptas were finally able to win permission to leave from their chief. He was reluctant but very proud to have his people included on such an important mission. He had accompanied his warriors on a daring hike to the base of the cliff and was immensely impressed with the massive rock wall guarding their forest. He was even more honored to climb the great tree used by the team to reach the heights. The chief was persuaded to cross the swinging bridge built by the Sularians to stand on the solid rock to gaze in awe at the land below. Now he too was as brave a warrior as Grush! His tribesmen were awed by their chief's courage. He was truly a great leader.

After one last feast and prolonged farewells, the Sularians set out for their return to base camp. The way back was easily accomplished over the now well traveled route so laboriously taken the first time by the small party of which Mark, Scagen, and Kayla had been members. They had all learned much from this assignment. Mark hoped his discoveries would offset any reprimands due from his impulsive act leading to the necessity of a rescue team for him.

About The Author

★★★★

Mary Starner, now a retired teacher, grew up in Connecticut. When she and her husband grew tired of muggy summers, mosquitos and endless sludgy winters they moved to Palo Alto, California to raise their three daughters. She accepted a position in the Los Altos, California schools. At that time, as part of the fourth grade language arts curriculum students were required to write a paragraph a day to share with the class. One day after something suddenly startled them all, Mrs. Starner suggested they each write an explanation of what had happened saying she would do that too. The class liked her version so much they wanted more. This led to this series of books that begins with *An Unexpected Beginning*. After several rejections from publishers she set the manuscripts aside, but even after all these years, someone from that group will still ask if her books were ever published.

Made in the USA
San Bernardino, CA
04 February 2017